Born and raised in Cork, Ireland, Michelle O'Sullivan completed her B.A. at University College Cork, in 2003, where she achieved joint honours in math and geography. From here, she travelled to the UK, where she attended Keele University and completed her Teacher Training in 2006. Originally a secondary school math teacher, she only remained in secondary for a short time, as she discovered her love of teaching lay elsewhere. Again she returned to Ireland, where she completed her masters in Teaching and Learning in Further and Higher Education. For many years afterwards she taught primary aged children, enjoying the diverse curriculum at this level. She now teaches in Further Education where she utilises the skills gained from her masters. Teaching and learning are a true passion of hers and she wants to help young minds realise their full potential, as she has.

To my family, thank you for your love, support and believing in my writing ability.

Michelle O' Sullivan

THE UNFORESEEABLE

AUSTIN MACAULEY PUBLISHERS™

LONDON • CAMBRIDGE • NEW YORK • SHARJAH

A CIP catalogue record for this title is available from the British Library.

ISBN 9781398412965 (Paperback)
ISBN 9781398413078 (ePub e-book)

www.austinmacauley.com

First Published 2022
Austin Macauley Publishers Ltd®
1 Canada Square
Canary Wharf
London
E14 5AA

To Austin Macauley Publishers, for taking a chance on an unknown author, thank you.

Prologue

The man stood on the edge of the cliff, looking at something no one else could see – well, after all – he was alone. He had climbed up those jagged rocks and grassy, steep verge hours earlier, wrestling with the weight of the decision that would change their lives forever. He closed his eyes, inhaled deeply and exhaled deeply, he knew what he had to do. He stared one final time into the expanse of sea and jagged rocks below and then let go.

Chapter 1

"Chrissy, let's go, Mr Thompson is going to be furious if we're late for math again, it'll be detention for sure," urged Jess. Jess was 15 but acted much older; she was the kind of girl you'd imagine in a plaid two-piece matching skirt set with black, square-framed glasses resting on the end of her nose, wispy blond hair caught in a bun at the back of her head – not a strand out of place – and a voice, sharp and crisp, that demanded attention. This depiction is fairly accurate but instead of the plaid suit the girls donned their black school pinafores embellished with the Tyneside crest above the left breast pocket, and as for her voice, the only person it demanded attention from was Chrissy, Jess' best friend. The girls had been inseparable since their first day of middle school. Jess had been a quiet, bookish type whilst Chrissy in contrast was a bit of a rebel – the pink and blue hair at the time, just an inkling of the personality that lay beneath.

Chrissy had been new, having transferred from St Lawrence's, but ever since her arrival the girls had made an instant connection, drawing together like a moth to a flame, or two parts of a magnet: positive and negative fused together.

"Oh math, math," she muttered. "I'm sure Mr Thompson will survive."

"But I won't if I get another detention. Mum was furious last time and took my phone away for a week," Jess pleaded.

"Oh, come on then, Miss Goody two shoes. Let's go before you have a complete meltdown," she teased.

Relieved, Jess picked up her bag from the floor, grabbed Chrissy's arm and raced towards the classroom, Chrissy in tow, just in time.

"Nice of you to join us girls, please take your seats," stated Mr Thompson before turning to face the class. "Circle geometry is all about remembering facts and formulae," stated Mr Thompson. "Can anyone impress me by reminding us about what we've learned thus far? Yes, Miss Perkins."

Of course, Jess would remember, Chrissy thought. Not that she herself didn't; she knew full well that the diameter was twice the radius and that the diameter times π gave the circumference of a circle, but no way was she volunteering this information to the entire class.

"Correct, Miss Perkins, well done. Today then, we shall be looking at tangents to a circle, which intersect perpendicularly to the circle's diameter," continued Mr Thompson.

"Oh, riveting," muttered Chrissy as she turned to Jess saying, "Wake me when it's time to leave, will you?"

Jess was only half-listening, however, because math was one of her favourite lessons and the fact that the 22-year-old, hotty, Mr Thompson taught it, had no bearing on the situation whatsoever. Besides, this routine between Jess and Chrissy had long been established. Chrissy would nap and Jess would nudge her awake whenever necessary; how the girl learnt anything still flummoxed Jess but despite her rebellious nature, Chrissy was as smart, if not smarter than Jess.

Chapter 2

"Mr Thompson is so hot, um, I mean clever." Jess flushed.

"No, you said what you meant the first time. Mr Thompson is so hot!" Chrissy teased, fanning herself with her hand lest she swoon.

"Stop it!" Yelled Jess, now a little more than embarrassed.

"You really must get over these crushes, you know, it'll never happen, he's way too old for you and…"

"He's not old, he's mature," interrupted Jess with a hint of indignation in her voice.

"I've got just the thing to cure you of your infatuation, and trust me this is gonna work."

"Oh yeah?" Jess urged, "What's that then?"

"Him," stated Chrissy, almost triumphantly as she turned her phone towards Jess.

Chrissy placed the phone on the lunch table so Jess could get a better look. She beamed from ear to ear, staring expectantly at her friend, waiting for her reaction.

"So who is he?" asked Jess.

"I hoped you'd want to know. Okay, remember the other day when I told you that I'd started seeing this guy – Pete?"

"Yea."

"Well, this is his cousin, Joe – he's 18; well, nearly, his birthday's in three months," stated Chrissy, matter-of-factly.

"Woah! Hold on, 18? I can't date an 18-year-old," protested Jess.

"But you can daydream about a 22-year-old teacher? Come on Jess, get real, at least this one could actually work," chastised Chrissy.

Jess was a little taken aback by the harshness of her friend's words but then she never was one to mince her thoughts or words to save the feelings of others – she said what she thought – it was one of the things Jess liked most about her friend.

"Okay, let's do it. I presume you want us to get together and double date?" queried Jess.

"Well, yea, eventually that's the idea, but you don't even know if you like each other yet silly," teased Chrissy, "but you'll find out tonight."

"Tonight?"

"Yea, you're meeting him tonight, it's all arranged – you're welcome!"

"What? You've already arranged it? Without speaking to me about it first?" Jess began to hyperventilate and the colour began to drain from her cheeks.

"Here, take this." Chrissy handed her the now-empty bag which had contained her lunch. "Just breathe silly, it'll all be fine, you'll see."

Chapter 3

The breathing techniques had been helpful. At first, when his wife had suggested the App, he had thought it to be a load of wishy-washy mumbo jumbo like those other spiritual and meditative Apps she uses, but to his surprise it had done the trick – his mind was clear, unencumbered, free of the turmoil which until now had given him, and his lovely wife, so many restless nights of late, nights spent tossing and turning and researching on his laptop. Now that he was clear-minded again, he knew exactly what to do. Step 1: delete his internet search history, it would be all too easy for the police to catch him out if they got a hold of his search history – total amateur hour. Okay, okay, he had never done anything like this before, had never needed to, but there comes a time when a man's gotta do what a man's gotta do. This was one of those times. Step 2: Plan. The devil is in the detail – that's what his father had always taught him. He could almost hear him now. "Fail to plan and plan to fail." No way could he risk that; this had to be perfect and implemented flawlessly, no room for error. He sat at his desk, removed a hardback jotter from the drawer and began to write.

Chapter 4

"Hey, you." He kissed her hello. "You look gorgeous as always."

"Thanks Pete, you look pretty great yourself," replied Chrissy, before returning his kiss.

Pete was approximately 5' 8", had sandy brown hair, was relatively well built for a 17-year-old and had a tiny scar above his lip from where he'd cut himself shaving. To Chrissy, he was perfect.

Jess stood nervously beside her, wearing skinny blue jeans, a short-cropped top covered with a light, baby-pink jacket. She kept glancing from Chrissy to Pete wondering where Joe was, and was now nervously twiddling the lower strands of her hair, which now hung loosely around her face.

"Hi. I'm Pete. You must be Jess? Chrissy's told me so much about you." Pete extended his hand by way of greeting. *So formal,* Jess thought, but shook it and smiled all the same.

"Where's your cousin?" She asked.

"Oh yea, sorry, he texted me, he's running late but should be here soon. Oh speak of the devil, here he is now."

Jess turned in the direction Pete was pointing and froze, he was even more handsome in person. He wore faded black jeans, a black leather jacket and his chiselled tone and tanned skin, really appealed to Jess.

"How are you mate?" Pete asked as the two-hugged hello.

"Yea good, not too bad," he replied. "Sorry, I'm late," he said, this time looking directly at Jess.

"No bother mate, it's all good. Well, now that you're here we'll leave you to it – Chrissy, let's leave these two to get acquainted, shall we?"

Pete and Chrissy turned to leave but as they did, Chrissy turned towards Jess, winked, and mouthed the words – have fun! Then they were gone.

They stood there alone, smiling at each other before Joe suggested they go for a walk around the park. They spoke about all sorts of things; he had this way of making her nerves disappear and he listened to her, like really listened, like what she had to say was the most important thing in the world so when he reached for her hand she didn't hesitate, and later when he kissed her and offered to walk her home, she thought of how lucky she was, how chivalrous he was. Already her mind was flooded with thoughts of their future, of double dates. Okay, maybe he was a little older than her but girls mature faster right, so maybe in that respect they were the same age; at least that's what she told herself. It's perfect – he's perfect!

Chapter 5

Finally, it was the weekend, thought Mr Thompson, not that he didn't love his job, he did, but it wasn't quite the same, not since he'd been forced to leave Berkshire Academy last year. He'd loved it there, it had been his first placement and when they'd offered him a permanent position, he couldn't believe his luck – he accepted there and then. The school was 2-form entry with a little over 600 pupils, each one donning a well-to-do parent powerhouse. These were your political, highbrow business types that expected nothing less than perfection from their children. Dave hadn't been fazed by that at all, in fact he thrived under such a challenge but it had all gone horribly wrong after he'd offered private tuition, if only he'd known then what he knew now.

Berkshire Academy wasn't what it appeared, this well-to-do area with its academy for the rich and powerful of tomorrow was merely a facade and its murky undertone had sucked Dave in and almost drowned him. Had it not been for his friend Byron, who got the charges dismissed, he was sure the outcome would have been quite different – no teacher can survive that sort of publicity, especially so scandalous. So now, here he was teaching at Tyneside, preparing children for GCSEs, it's approach to T&L (Teaching and Learning) so far apart from what had gone before, yet that was okay, he'd resigned himself to that fact and this job allowed him to breathe, to take stock of his life and focus on what really mattered; if he'd learnt anything from the incident, he'd learnt that a job was solely to pay the bills, whilst it may have once consumed his every thought, been the sparkle in his eye that was gone, that was merely a shadow of his former self.

It had only been three months after the incident that he'd met her – Beth, by sheer accident. Byron had told him, ordered him, to go to the gym to let some steam off, he'd said, and he had – he'd pounded the treadmill and given Bradley Wiggins a good run for his money on the bike. He'd felt better for it so when the water cascaded upon him from the shower afterwards, he'd felt lighter, like a weight had been lifted off of his shoulders. He towelled, dressed, packed up his belongings and then checked his mobile, like he always did, before leaving the changing room. The message was from Byron and the words hit him like a wrecking ball. He stumbled backwards just managing to make the bench before collapsing upon it, staring still at the message on his screen.

'It' s over buddy. All charges have been dropped. You' re in the clear. It' s finally over – you (we) should celebrate. '

He stared, dumbfounded, at the message, reading and re-reading. It was finally over, no more sideward glances from colleagues, whisperings in the staffroom, death threats from parents or vulgarities left in his classroom by students. He'd been cleared, better than that, charges had been dropped which meant there was no case, nothing to clear him of. It was at that precise moment that he realised how naive he'd actually been, still was; things would never go back to what they were, not at this school, he'd have to move.

A new start, a fresh start, he told himself as he left the changing room to the gym and that's when he saw her, his Beth, all-athletic and toned in her yoga kit. They locked eyes, only for a moment, and smiled at each other and then she was gone. Their relationship didn't start there, of course, but that was the day they'd first met. Although, a few short weeks later, after myriad dates and endless hours of conversation, they were officially a couple and a mere eight months after that, they were happily married. His Beth, so supportive and in love that she too had uprooted her life and relocated to Tyneside with him.

At first, it had been rough, commuting to see each other and then finally her move which meant they were both surviving, somehow, on his salary alone until she was settled and got a job. But settle she did, in fact she flourished. She rented a room at a nearby fitness studio and taught yoga. Fliers had been put up all over town and even she was surprised by the uptake. One of the local mums, a governor at Tyneside, had even secured her a job at Tyneside School stating that it would be wonderful for the children's fitness and wellbeing. Of course, Mr Mc Alistair (the Headmaster) agreed and so she began the very next term.

Everything had worked out for the better – 'Everything happens for a reason,' as his mum would always say. This little backwater town had become their home. They were happy here but yet something was niggling at him, the thought always just out of reach. It would formulate in his mind but just as he would focus on it, it would dissipate and was gone.

Just like that, there but not there. So, Mr Thompson was glad that it was the weekend, where he could focus on one thing, anything other than what lay lurking in the dark recesses of his mind.

Chapter 6

'It's official,' she wrote. 'We're officially dating. It's been only two weeks since that first night at the park but we clicked, you know. We've seen each other so many times since then too, some that even Chrissy doesn't know about, not cos I don't wanna tell her, I tell her everything, but like when am I meant to tell her if I'm always with Joe?

'We've been to the park again, a lot, it's become our favourite place, cos you know, it's where it all started and that. We've been other places too: the arcade, the shopping mall, the pier and cafe. He's super sweet, he mostly pays for everything, not that I want him to, I've got my own money but he's like, 'Babe, I've got this' and the way he says it makes me all warm inside, like he'll protect me you know, keep me safe and love me forever. He's also so, oh what's the word...chivalry — no, chivalrous, like men are supposed to be, like they are in those romcoms I watch with Mum.

'She'd like him too, I know she would, but I haven't told her about him yet. For now, I just want to keep him all to myself. Oh, I guess I can't, well not quite. I've just remembered we've got our double date this Friday with Chrissy and Pete. That'll be nice though, to finally get together, all four of us. It should've happened ages ago but let's just say that things between Chrissy and Pete have been somewhat rocky, but they must've sorted things out if we're meeting. Anyway, watch this space I guess...

'Joe has just messaged me: SWEET DREAMS MY LOVELY 😚 I swear that boy knows exactly how to melt my heart. Well better sleep A.K.A. text Joe.

'Night.'

Chapter 7

The sun shone gloriously overhead, the heat like that of a sunbed beating down upon them as they bargained for possession. The score was already 3–2 to the opposing team and tensions were high, least of all from Mrs Brickman who was shouting at the girls from the side-line.

Jess had never really understood lacrosse but Chrissy had informed her it was a lot like netball. There are ten players on each lacrosse team (okay, so not entirely like netball), four players must stay on the defensive half of the field and three players must stay on the offensive half and three players can go anywhere on the field. This, as she was told, was Chrissy's position – can you really see me anywhere else, not constantly involved in all of the action, her friend had said. Jess had laughed at this; that's exactly where her friend would be, in the thick of the action.

There were two halves to the game, each half consisting of two quarters and each quarter lasted 12 minutes. The game starts with a face off, basically the ball starts on the ground and a player from each team grapples for possession. That had been today's first failing, Tyneside had failed to gain possession. The second had been when one of Tyneside's players, a girl called Jane, had illegally body checked one of the opposition's players and so again the school had lost valuable possession. So, here they were in the last few minutes of the second quarter and down by one.

"Come on, Tyneside," she yelled from the bleachers, maybe some encouragement was what they needed, Jess thought as she began to cheer louder. Although, Jess believed that Mrs Brickman was giving the team enough 'encouragement' to last them all season.

Jess' phone buzzed in her pocket, she retrieved it and held it to her ear but the reception was terrible – then they were gone. Weird, she thought, as she looked to see who the caller had been, an unknown number. She assumed it must have been a wrong number as she returned her phone to her pocket but the words still chilled her to the bone. It had sounded like the caller said, 'I'm watching you!'

Cheers and whoops erupted from the field. Tyneside was now level with Rocksdale and only a minute till half time, it was just the break they needed. Jess was on her feet too now whooping and cheering along with the others but as she sat back down, there he was – beside her.

Chapter 8

"Oh, what a game," exclaimed Chrissy in the locker room. "You really did us proud, Luc, without that last goal we were goosed. Three cheers for Lucy. Hip, hip."

"Hooray!" they chorused.

"Hip, hip."

"Hooray!"

"Hip, hip."

"Hooray!"

By this point, Lucy was now practically crowd surfing above six of the girls' heads.

"Put her down girls," demanded the authoritative voice of Mrs Brickman, who had now appeared in the locker room doorway. "What were you girls trying to do out there, give me a heart attack? That win was far too close and Jane, an illegal body check? You know better than that!"

"But Miss..." Roxy interjected.

"No, but Miss, young lady. I do not tolerate underhanded play, we're above that, *we're ladies*."

The girls giggled at this, this was Mrs Brickman's motto, both on and off the field: foul play – no, we're ladies; cheating in an exam – never, we're ladies; getting into the world's biggest fight and pulling each other's hair whilst trying to gouge each other's eyes out, absolutely not – we're ladies! Mrs Brickman briskly turned and left the girls to shower and bask in their success but parting words floated from her lips, "Well done for saving our bacon, Lucy."

Chapter 9

"Where did you come from?" She beamed.

"Well, literally, the tree line," he joked.

She elbowed him gently in the ribs to show that's not what she meant but that she enjoyed the teasing.

"You told me last night that Chrissy had a game. I was free, so I thought I'd come surprise you," answered Joe.

"Well, you certainly did that, I'm so glad you're here," she said as she kissed and hugged him hello.

She could sense some of the other girls staring at her. You know, that feeling you get when someone is trying to burn a hole in the back of your head, that's how it felt. She considered suggesting that they leave but then thought, no, why should they? Those other girls were just jealous so instead she intertwined her fingers amongst Joe's and then wrapped her free arm around his muscular bicep as she perched her head upon his shoulder.

"I'm so glad, you're here," she whispered.

"You said that already, but I know what you mean. I'm glad I'm here too."

Jess spent the whole of half-time explaining the rules of lacrosse to Joe; she was now somewhat of an expert. So by the third and fourth quarter, they were both frantically screaming at the Tyneside players, encouragingly, of course. The score was level at 12-12 and it looked as if the Tyneside players were beginning to tire. One of Rocksdale's players was headed straight for goal, which would lead to Tyneside's certain defeat, but Chrissy had body checked her and gained possession. She caught Lucy's eye and passing the ball, it majestically soared through the air and next into the back of the net. Tyneside, by some miracle, had won.

Joe had suggested that they wait for Chrissy but Jess knew better than to do that. First, the team would take ages in the showers and second of all, they, the team, would celebrate together.

"So just us then, eh?" he queried.

"Yea, guess so. Is that okay?"

"It's more than okay," he answered, as he swept her up and enveloped her in another heart-stopping kiss.

"So, pizza?" Jess suggested as he released her.

He nodded. "Pizza."

Chapter 10

Nothing much happened for the rest of the week; well not unless you count a fight in the cafeteria and a math test on calculus. Mr Thompson had been acting unusual though, Jess hadn't quite known how to phrase it. "He's just off, don't you think?"

She eyeballed Chrissy, whose hair was now purple, to see if she too had noticed it.

"Yea, I guess. He's definitely not himself, he's all moody and serious and like, 'Miss Ramsdale, please focus on your own test.' That poor girl wouldn't cheat if her life depended on it," remarked Chrissy.

"He's jumpier too. Remember the other day, in the middle of his explanation about the derivative, when Mr Morley knocked on the door..."

Chrissy couldn't help but erupt into laughter.

"Oh, stop it," she pleaded, it's making my sides hurt.

"It's not funny," Jess protested.

"Oh, it was, his face went ashen and the way he stumbled backwards into the board, it was hilarious. I wish we'd that on video. I could do with the cash from Candid camera."

"I guess it was kinda funny, but that poor man, he must have gotten a terrible fright to react the way he did," stated Jess. "And his car's been here late every night too."

"Oh, has it now?" asked Chrissy, suddenly very serious and intrigued. "And how would you know that, spying on him are you?"

"Don't be ridiculous," admonished Jess. "It's just strange is all. I wonder what's going on."

"Okay, Miss Marple, can we please now forget about Mr Thompson. He's so last term's news and we have a double date to get ready for."

The girls grabbed the remaining items needed from their respective lockers and left the school arm in arm, joyfully chatting about the evening that lay ahead. Neither of them noticed the man watching them from the school car park, where once again Mr Thompson's car remained parked.

Chapter 11

Everyone was in high spirits. It had been decided earlier in the week that they would play crazy golf, much to Joe's delight because he was an expert, or so he liked to boast. Turned out he was pretty good, albeit a little bit of a cheat. Every time it was Jess' turn he would 'accidentally' stop the ball with his foot. Jess didn't mind though; at least it would give her an excuse when she didn't win later and it's not like she was really very good at the game anyway.

Even Pete and Chrissy seemed to be enjoying themselves, smiling carefree and wrapped in each other's arms between shots. It somehow reached time for the final hole, time had drifted by so quickly, where an uphill slope of blue faced Jess. The aim was to hit the ball towards the top and somehow manage to get it into the open mouth of a shark, whose expectant mouth kept opening and closing, without having it roll back down the hill.

The others had gone before her and scored a: 5, 4 and 4 – it was a par 2. There would be no interference from Joe this time due to the inclined slope. She positioned her ball, steadied her club, took aim and…where was her ball? It hadn't come back. Expressions and comments of disbelief ensued – she had scored a hole in one! The first of the night and on the toughest hole.

"Well done, babe," Joe said as he placed a congratulatory kiss on her lips. "Maybe I should've let you play properly all night? We'll have to come back, just the two of us for a rematch."

"I'd like that." She beamed, reaching for his hand.

Afterwards, they'd all walked along the pier, ate sugared donuts and chatted nonchalantly. Jess wasn't sure how it'd begun but something had happened whilst she and Joe were queuing for chips.

"What's up, mate?" Joe asked, his question directed at Pete.

"She's what's up, she's doing my bleeding head in."

Jess turned to look at Chrissy, whom it was clear had now been crying for quite some time.

"Don't speak about my friend like that. What have you done to her, Pete? Look at her, she's in a right state," asked Jess, protectively putting an arm around her very distraught friend as she sat beside her on the bench.

"Shut up, Jess, you don't know what the hell you're talking about!" Pete spat back.

"Woah mate, I think it's time for us to leave, yea?" motioned Joe as he guided Pete away.

Jess was left holding one large bag of chips whilst cradling a hysterical Chrissy. Now was not the time to ask what had happened. So instead she said, "Chips?"

Chrissy looked up and both girls ate without sharing another word.

Chapter 12

Tonight was crazy! It went from being crazy good to crazy bad. What the hell happened? Chrissy and Pete have fought before but nothing like that. that was intense. Thank goodness Joe was there or things could've gotten a whole lot worse. I hope he's okay — Joe that is. I've texted him since I've gotten home but so far, nothing. Please, God, let him be okay.

(I don't care about Pete; he can suffer for the way he treated Chrissy. If she takes him back after this...)

Chapter 13

Jess woke with a start, her diary balancing precariously on the edge of her duvet. She placed it on her dresser and instinctively picked up her phone to read the message that Joe had sent her during the night, but there was none. An ache developed in the pit of her stomach. Pete better not have taken his anger out on Joe or so help her God she'd make him sorry, she thought.

She pressed the button to dial his number and held the phone to her ear. It was ringing; in her bedroom. Of course, he'd handed it to her last night whilst he paid for the chips and she'd put it in her jacket pocket forgetting to return it to him once everything started kicking off. That's why he hadn't replied to her. Relief washed over her and sleep overcame her; his phone would have to wait.

It was 11:30 when she finally re-awoke. She showered, dressed, ate breakfast and headed towards the garage to return Joe's phone. She removed it from her jacket pocket and switched the screen on, just to check the battery, not that she was spying but the text on the screen stopped her dead.

'Thanks for getting me outta there mate, she was doing my nut in. So bloody moody and demanding.

Well, it's done now anyway, cos there's someone else so u don't have to worry. Thanks again. I owe u.'

As if there was any doubt Jess peered to the sender's name: Pete.

Chapter 14

Furious, Jess stormed into the garage. Joe, seeing her, smiled in hello but his smile quickly faded when he saw the scour upon her face.

"What's up?" he asked.

"You tell me," she bit back as she thrust the phone towards his chest.

Reading the message currently still displayed on the screen he merely replied, "Oh, I see."

"Oh, you see, do you? Well, that's just great," and she turned and left.

Joe was left standing, perplexed, Pete had a lot to answer for.

Chapter 15

It had been a week since Jess' fight with Joe and yet Jess couldn't bring herself to apologise, despite how guilty she felt about the whole thing. She knew it wasn't Joe's fault, from the very beginning he'd tried to de-escalate the situation, yet in her fury, she'd laid all of the blame at his feet. It wasn't surprising then to see that now she was moping the corridors, glazed over in lessons and even her friendship with Chrissy had altered. The world, for her, had lost its sparkle and she longed, more than anything to get it back.

The following morning she had woken up a little bit more optimistic, gotten out of the right side of the bed as it were. She had chided herself about her stupidity and her immaturity the previous night. She had decided that enough was enough and was determined to shake herself free of the funk she was in.

Walking to school, a warm summer breeze surrounding her like a warm embrace, and the traces of a smile emerging on her lips, she felt re-energised. She quickened her step, this time walking more purposefully – yes, it would be a better day. Or it had been until she met Chrissy.

"I just don't get him, ya know? We were fine and then he just goes and blows up, saying all this stuff to me and I'm like, 'Woah where'd all that come from?'"

Jess had had this same conversation with Chrissy at least a half a dozen times since that fateful night. It was like Chrissy was stuck in a loop, going over and over again, forced to relive the same maddening moments again and again.

"I know, it's not fair. Look, he's a jerk, you're better off without him," said Jess, comfortingly.

"He is, and it's not like I want him back or anything, I ABSOLUTELY DO NOT, but I just want to understand, ya know?"

Jess did understand; Chrissy needed closure and without it, she feared her friend would never move on. Trouble was, Pete hadn't responded to any of Chrissy's messages and Jess feared he never would.

The tests lay on their desks as they entered the math room. Jess had been so distracted looking at that that she had almost sat on the beautiful yellow rose that had been placed on her seat. Furtively, she put it in her bag, now was not the time. She glanced back at the test paper on her desk as she took her seat, 98%. Stupidly, she'd forgotten to calculate one of the derivatives; she wouldn't make that mistake again.

Soon enough, the bell rang for the end of the day. She packed up her stuff and headed for the library, throwing herself into her work was exactly the distraction she needed right now. She hadn't heard from Joe all week and whilst she knew it was her fault he could have at least text her.

First on the hit list was Mr Larson's essay on 'The advancements in medicine since the Middle Ages'. Oh yeah, she thought because that isn't broad at all. Jess sat there contemplating where to start…she would make a list:

- The Plague (Black Death)
- Florence Nightingale
- Cowpox and Smallpox

She had an eerie feeling that someone was watching her but besides the librarian the room was empty. The library backed onto the school car park but short of a few cars, it, too, was deserted. *It's not like any teacher is going to be spying on me,* she told herself. Now, feeling foolish, she resumed her list.

- Edward Jenner and the invention of penicillin
- Victorian medicine
- Hypocrates – the Hippocratic oath
- Autopsies

She checked out a book which detailed how modern medicine is nowadays often hindered due to religious or cultural beliefs and then found a fascinating article about a mother who had been imprisoned for neglect when she failed to seek medical treatment for her child. She wrote down the reference for the article and tagged it as a favourite so she could later return to it.

A noise, a shuffling, caught her attention and she realised it was already 17:30. Ms Sharp, the librarian, was retrieving her belongings.

"Sorry Miss, I hadn't realised the time."

"Oh that's alright, it was nice to see you so engrossed. I was reluctant to disturb you," replied the ever-helpful Ms Sharp.

Books in hand, Jess left the library and turned to leave, nearly colliding with Mr Thompson.

"Oh, sorry sir, I was miles away."

"No harm, Miss Perkins. Great score on that test, oh and enjoy your rose," he said, as he continued walking towards his car, almost as if the near collision hadn't happened and he, too, was preoccupied.

Chapter 16

"I was thinking we'd have fish for dinner, what do you think?" Beth queried.

"Hmmm," he mused.

"Dave, are you even listening?" she asked, slight irritation in her voice. He had been like this for a while now – distant, preoccupied.

"Sorry love, what did you ask? I'm listening now."

"I asked whether you wanted fish for dinner," she repeated.

"Yes, fish would be lovely, thank you. Do you need any help?"

"No, I've got it. You may as well go get some marking done," she offered.

"Then I'll do that," he replied, marking the furthest thing from his mind.

Chapter 17

Another week had gone by and Chrissy was all but transformed – her hair now pink with blue tips and her exuberant smile once more affixed to her face. She had wiped the slate clean of Pete and had left that baggage at the airport, well, figuratively speaking anyway. Winning the lacrosse league had helped too; with all the extra training Mrs Brickman had made the team endure, it had kept her distracted, and that was all the distraction Chrissy had needed to heal. Now she was back, the new and improved Chrissy – Chrissy 2.0

Things were looking up for Jess too. First, a rose, then chocolates, Joe really was trying to make an effort. She would message him soon. She missed him and it was obvious now that he'd forgiven her; that was the purpose of his gifts she supposed, to let her know that things would be okay from now on, that they'd be okay?

Chapter 18

It was happening again. Mr Thompson could sense it. The sideways glances in the corridors, or worse, the colleagues that averted their eyes when they passed him. He was growing distant even from Beth, whom he barely spoke a word to the other night at dinner, but even she had grown silent when he walked into the staffroom this lunchtime. He couldn't bear it. Something had to be done.

Chapter 19

He arose the next morning, early, his body full of anticipation. Another week had rolled by and he'd waited long enough. Kissing his sleeping wife goodbye, he stealthily slipped downstairs: it wouldn't do to wake her now.

He drank his black coffee, its warmth instantly fuelling his weary limbs. 45 minutes and the hardware store would be open, this had been one of the things he'd searched online. He relished the last remaining remnants of his coffee, wrote a loving, explanatory note to his wife and left.

The journey to the next town was mundane but one that had to be completed to achieve his objective. He couldn't afford to be complacent now. There it was, as Google maps said it was. The store was old-fashioned, one of those family run places and smelt of sawdust. He browsed the aisles looking for what he needed.

"Can I help you sir?" asked a gentleman who looked to be in his early seventies.

The voice had startled him but he politely replied, "Oh, good morning, yes, I'm looking for cable ties – you know, to tie back plants or some such."

The gentleman directed him to the necessary aisle and when he returned to the counter, cable ties in hand, the gentleman spoke once more, "Not seen you around these parts before, I never forget a face."

"No, I'm not from around here but the wife wanted these and you were the earliest store open so I surmised the sooner we start the sooner we finish, so here I am. How much do I owe you?"

"Ah, a man of action, I like that," he replied, whilst placing the ties in a paper bag. "That'll be 76p, please."

"Right you are," he said whilst paying and simultaneously cursing himself for choosing this store. The man's words replayed in his mind – I never forget a face – *great,* he thought.

"Have a great day now and regards to your wife," said the elderly gentleman as his customer left the store.

"And to you, sir." He waved as he left. Maybe the man would remember his face, but maybe, just maybe, he would remember his pleasant demeanour too and tell the police that this man couldn't possibly have done what they were claiming.

Chapter 20

It was still early when he arrived at the house but any moment now he knew his target would be in sight. They wouldn't suspect a thing but rather, be totally ambushed, caught unawares. Soon, very soon, they would be in the boot of his car and this *situation* would get resolved.

He wasn't naive enough to believe that this would be easy but he'd prepared for it. He'd been watching the house for weeks; knew their routines and at this hour, on a Saturday morning, their street was all but deserted; finally, if there was a struggle he was prepared for that too. He'd purchased some dichloromethane, or chloroform as it's more commonly known, online. It had been surprisingly cheap too, he'd thought, at £11.95. So, he was all set. Now, all he had to do was wait and his prey would walk right by him.

He didn't have to wait long…A wicked smile etched its way across his mouth. He doused the cloth in chloroform and readied himself to leave the safety of his car. The boot had previously been popped open for easy access and his driver's window had been rolled down – it wouldn't do to inadvertently render himself unconscious.

Within seconds of passing him, he was upon them, cloth around their mouth and dragging them backwards towards the boot. That part was a little clumsy but he was no hardened criminal. His plan had worked and that's what mattered.

Apparently, there's an exact science to the dosage of chloroform, something about the dosage and the victims or patient's body weight. Give too little and the person could regain consciousness, too much and they could die, so he'd figured the more the better, just in case, and he was sure they were still breathing when he closed the boot. However, now he realised they were loose in the boot. In his haste to get away, he'd forgotten to use the cable ties which now laughed mockingly at him from the passenger seat. Luckily, the road he was travelling was isolated and deserted enough for him to stop. Bringing the car to a halt, he grabbed the cable ties and made for the rear of the car. He paused, steeling himself for what he knew he had to do. Somewhat anxiously, he opened the boot, praying he'd used enough chloroform, and hog-tied the unconscious body inside, sealing their fate once more as he closed the boot and resumed driving.

Chapter 21

Jess awoke with a stale taste in her mouth. Her limbs were stiff and her back ached. She tried to stretch but was unable to. Her eyes adjusted to her surroundings and fear engulfed her – this was not her bedroom.

She tried to recall how she'd gotten here. Tried to recall her last memory, but nothing. Now, too, her head ached and her thoughts were muddled. Desperately, she called out for help but her throat was dry and her voice came out as a hoarse plea. She swallowed to try and produce enough spittle in her mouth, then, screamed once more, twice more…but nobody came.

Chapter 22

The cottage was remote and surrounded by woodland. Ordinarily, it was a picturesque setting: wild flowers, woodland animals and a pottering of birch, beech and cedar trees, best of all it was miles from anywhere so the perfect location for a private getaway.

The cottage had been in his family for generations. On numerous occasions, he'd suggested they get away from it all and take a vacation here but life had always gotten in the way. Yet, here he was now, on a vacation of sorts, his prisoner in the other room screaming incessantly.

"Oh just shut up," he replied in response to their cries of desperation. "No one can hear you and no one is coming."

Chapter 23

It had to be at least lunchtime, Jess mused. She had watched the sunlight pass from the left to the right of the window of the room she was in but still she was alone. She had screamed until her throat was raw and now it felt like she'd swallowed razor blades. At one point, she'd thought that she'd heard someone reply. Instantly, she'd frozen, partly with fear but partly with the hope of salvation, listening acutely for any sound, any sign of movement but the place was as silent as before.

She racked her brain trying to remember what had happened but hunger pangs reminded her she needed to eat. *Okay,* she thought, *let's start there. Yesterday, Friday, what did school serve for lunch?* Then she had a sickening thought. How long had she been gone? Was it Saturday? That had been the catalyst for the dam gates bursting wide open. Her brain was flooded with questions. Who had taken her? When had they taken her? Where had they taken her? But the question that unnerved her, more than any other, was...Why had they taken her?

What did they want from her? The fear consumed her. She could feel her muscles contracting. Her breathing quickening. *No,* she told herself, *pull it together, you cannot fall apart now. Find something to fix your gaze on and just breathe.* She stared at the book on the dresser table, breathing in, then out, in, then out. It was working, her breathing was slowing. *You're doing it,* she told herself, *just keep breathing.*

She continued to focus on her breathing; a realisation dawned upon her, that book, it was familiar, and in that moment it all came flooding back to her.

Chapter 24

The man, whom earlier that morning had been confident and resolute about what it was he had to do was now having second thoughts. What man, what person, kidnaps another person rather than having a reasonable conversation?

A reasonable conversation, he scoffed at his own words. There was nothing reasonable about this, or anything that had happened leading to this moment. The rose, the chocolates, the notes, they had been in vain – leading to nothing. It was time for action.

Chapter 25

Saturday rolled into Sunday and Sunday into Monday. Jess had heard sounds, but still hadn't seen a soul. At some point, whilst she slept, her zip ties had been cut from around her wrists but her legs were still held in place, secured to each bedpost, a position that was painfully uncomfortable. She had searched, where she could, for something, anything to free herself but it was futile.

In addition to her hands being freed, food and water had also been left for her. She ate sparingly not knowing when her next meal would come but the smell was unbearable. She had wet herself at least three times now, unable to relieve herself in the toilet and no one coming to her assistance, no matter how much she pleaded. Her clothes were once again dry but yellowed and crusted and her skin, she felt, was raw from irritation.

Chapter 26

Two Days Previously – Friday

Jess was overwhelmed by the realisation. That book, she'd been carrying it when she'd been taken. Mr Thompson had gotten into his car and reversed to leave the car park when he'd been cut off. Putting his car back in gear, after it'd stalled, Mr Thompson drove away allowing *him* to grab her; hit her over the head (with that book); dump her in his boot; tie her up and drive off. She had kicked the boot the whole way there. Tried to force loose the taillights to allow herself to be able to put her hand through and attract attention, like they do in the movies, but nothing had worked. He had her. Pete had her.

Chapter 27

Saturday

Mr Perkins stormed into the room and stared down at the man he had secured in the chair. He had been worried about the robustness of the chair, being made from wood, but it had held firm against Dave's struggles.

"So Dave, or Mr Thompson, is it? How do you want to play this? Are you going to tell me what I want to know or do I have to beat it out of you?"

Mr Thompson's eyes were transfixed. He knew this man, what was going on? He tried to recall from where he knew him: the gym, the…then it hit him. He was Jess' father, they'd met at parents' evening.

"Mr Perkins, I don't understand what you want. Is it Jess?" queried Mr Thompson.

"Is it Jess? Is it Jess? Of course it's Jess. Why else would I be doing this?" challenged Mr Perkins.

Mr Thompson said nothing. He was frantically trying to determine why a parent would kidnap him. What motive could he possibly have? The rose and the chocolates…

Mr Thompson had been right; it was all happening again but not in the way he'd imagined. He realised now that it was not his livelihood that was in jeopardy but maybe his life.

"I know all about you Mr Thompson, I've done my research. I know how you left that other school, with your tail between your legs. Thought you'd hide out in our little town, did you? Thought us townies wouldn't see you for what you really are? We're wise to you Mr Thompson, let me tell you. What's the matter, your pretty little wife doesn't do it for you, you have to prey on young girls?"

The thought made him sick. Bile rose up from his stomach and erupted from his mouth landing all over the floor and on his shoes.

"I swear, if you've touched her, I'll kill you," he stated, wiping his mouth.

Mr Thompson hadn't interrupted the man once, thinking it wiser to let the man speak. It was obvious the man found him repulsive but he had to find a way to convince him otherwise.

"Well? Speak!" demanded Mr Perkins.

"Mr Perkins, I promise you I never touched your daughter, nor have I touched any of my students, nor would I."

Mr Perkins glared at the man sitting before him; such protestations – but were they true?

"You say you've done your research, correct?" He didn't wait for an answer. "Then, if you have, you'll know that the charges brought against me were dropped. I was never charged with anything," explained a desperate Mr Thompson.

"Just because you weren't charged doesn't mean you didn't do it," rebutted an agitated Mr Perkins.

"And that is the gloom that follows me around on a daily basis, the notion in people's heads that I did something wrong, something unforgivable."

"Oh, I'm meant to feel sorry for you, am I? You're the victim?" interrupted Mr Perkins, the irony of what he'd just said not lost on him but he would not let his little girl down.

"Mr Perkins, what is it you think I've done exactly, to Jess?"

"Seduced her, of course, with that bloody rose, those chocolates and those notes. But I intercepted those notes, she never saw a single one. So, sorry to spoil your little plan but it won't work this time," stated Mr Perkins somewhat triumphantly.

Mr Thompson sat silently for a very long time wondering how to explain to this man what he knew.

"Nothing to say?" Jeered Mr Perkins. "That's okay, we have time," and he walked out of the room and left him to his solitude.

Chapter 28
Monday

The next time Jess opened her eyes, he was sat, on a chair, beside the bed, within reaching distance of her. Her clothes had been changed but her restraints were still in place. She felt fresher but the thought that he'd undressed her made her skin crawl.

"Hello beautiful," he said, as he reached out to put a loose strand of hair behind her ear.

She involuntarily flinched and he laughed.

"I'm not going to hurt you – I love you," he chastised. "I only hit you with the book because you were refusing to come with me. I never wanted to hit you, that's the last thing I want."

Jess thought back to when Pete had dated Chrissy. How had they not seen how unhinged he was? *Chrissy has had a lucky escape,* she thought, and then uncontrollably she sobbed as she realised that she might not be as lucky.

Was anyone even looking for her? It was Monday, wasn't it? Mum and Dad would be frantic. She'd been due to stay at Chrissy's Friday and Saturday but surely they'd have worried when she didn't come home Sunday? And now it was

Monday, so now school would be worried too? Yes, people must be looking for her.

"People will be looking for me," she raged. "They'll wonder where I am."

"Oh, don't worry," he said. "I've texted them all for you. Your parents think you're with Chrissy and her family; Chrissy thinks that you're with Joe and Joe – well, it seems you've not been messaging each other for a while so I just left that one."

"You're a monster," she called.

"Now, come on. Would a monster send you roses? Chocolates? And write you love notes?" he questioned.

"They were from…" and she paused realising the mistake she'd made. "They were from you?"

"Of course. Oh? Did you think they were from Joe." He laughed.

Tears rolled in steady streams down her cheeks.

"Oh, come now, don't cry," he told her, but she refused to look at him and could not stop crying.

"Alright then, have it your way," he shouted, as he left her alone to cry. "After all I've done for you – so ungrateful!" He slammed the door shut, his anger once more evident.

I have to get out of here, she thought.

Chapter 29
Sunday

Mr Perkins had listened all morning to the insights of Mr Thompson and despite the overwhelming desire to protect his daughter, he was inclined to believe the man. The main reason being, all of the notes came during school time which is how Mr Perkins was able to intercept them, Jess was at school – but so too was Mr Thompson.

Mr Perkins had gotten it terribly wrong. He'd abducted a man he thought was pursuing his daughter but that hadn't been the case. Now, sitting beside him, he cut his bindings, freeing the man at last.

"Can I use your phone, please?" asked Mr Thompson.

"What?" Panic engulfed him as he was sure the other man was about to phone the police.

"Your phone. I need to ring my wife, she'll be out of her mind with worry."

Mr Perkins thought back to the note he'd left for his wife when it all began.

Gone fishing. Back Monday.
Don't worry. Love, Bill.

Don't worry, now all he could do was worry, what lay ahead for him now? He hadn't planned for after...

He handed Mr Thompson his phone and as he dialled and relayed the events of the past several hours to his wife, Mr Perkins once again employed his wife's breathing techniques – in, out, in, out.

Chapter 30
Monday

"Yes, this is Mrs Perkins."

"Hello, this is Ms Appleton, from Tyneside School. I'm ringing to confirm the whereabouts of your daughter, Jessica."

"She's at school." Obviously she's not, her subconscious told her, otherwise why would the school be ringing. "Isn't she?" questioned a nervous Mrs Perkins.

"I'm afraid not, Mrs Perkins. Her form tutor registered her absence this morning and she hasn't arrived since," replied Ms Appleton.

"Then where is she?" demanded Mrs Perkins, fear now creeping in.

"I was rather hoping that you could tell us Mrs Perkins. I wouldn't worry though, I'm sure there's a logical explanation."

Ms Appleton had tried to be as reassuring as possible but she knew by the time she had finished the conversation the woman on the other end of the line was a withering wreck.

In…, out…, in…, out…, slow deep breaths she reminded herself. Jess had spent all weekend at Chrissy's, perhaps both girls were just late and Mr or Mrs March were also receiving an equally distressing phone call from the school this morning. She searched her phone address book and dialled their home number. Mrs March, who like her own husband, worked from home, answered on the third ring.

"Hello."

"Hello, Mrs March, it's Mrs Perkins. I was just ringing to see if the girls are still at the house?"

"Heavens, no. Chrissy left over an hour ago," she replied after consulting her watch.

"And Jess?"

"I'm sorry?"

"Did Jess leave at the same time, with Chrissy?"

"Jess wasn't here. Why would Jess be here?" asked a confused Mrs March.

"Wasn't she with you and your family this weekend? In fact, since Friday evening?" asked a desperate Mrs Perkins.

There was a moment's silence on the other end of the line as a reluctant Mrs March answered, "I'm sorry, but no."

Mrs Perkins dropped to her knees, clutching the phone to her chest. She could hear mumblings on the other end of the phone but she was still trying to process the information she'd just been told – Jess had not been at the March's house! Raising the phone to her ear, she simply said, "I've got to go," and ended the call.

The police had been no help whatsoever. She had told them about the school phoning her when her daughter had failed to show up for school. Just another kid that doesn't want to go to school, they'd said. She'll return when she gets hungry, they'd said. There's nothing that we could do anyway until 24 hours have passed, they'd said. That was the moment that the placid Mrs Perkins had seen red.

"She's been missing for three to four days," she bellowed.

"Three to four days? I thought you said…" Mrs Perkins was transferred from switchboard to a Detective Inspector Jones. For the second time, she relayed what she could of her daughter's disappearance, which wasn't much.

"And what about Mr Perkins, any chance that your daughter could be with him?" proposed the detective.

"No, he's been fishing since Saturday and only returned last night."

"He went fishing after your daughter disappeared?"

"I told you, we, I didn't know she was missing until earlier this morning. My husband still doesn't know; I can't get a hold of him. Oh God, we're awful parents, how could we not know our daughter was missing?"

She broke down sobbing.

"Mrs Perkins, best thing you can do now is stay home and wait for your daughter there. I have your information, we'll be in touch."

Chapter 31
Monday

Mr Perkins was awakened Monday morning to a knocking on his front door. He glanced at the alarm clock beside the bed as he reached for his dressing gown – 10:07. As he opened the door and saw their uniforms, he'd have sworn that his heart skipped a beat. Dave had sworn to him he understood, had said that if he'd a daughter that he'd probably have acted similarly, had assured him that he himself didn't want any of the attention and publicity that something like this would cause, so, best to let bygones be bygones, he'd said; but now, he'd phoned the police. *Probably only said it to ensure his safe release – hindsight,* he'd thought.

"You'd better come in," he told the officers.

The police officers looked at each other and followed him inside.

"I suppose you'll want a statement?"

"A statement." This piqued the attention of the taller officer. Never had they had a member of the public volunteer a statement – had this man kidnapped his own daughter, his wife having no knowledge of the fact?

"Best get dressed and come with us, Mr Perkins."

Inside the police station Mr Perkins was handed over to a DI Jones.

"Sir, he's been rambling about a Mr Thompson, something about him liking his daughter."

"And how does this pertain to his missing daughter and his statement he's so keen to give?" Probed the D. I.

"Not sure sir, but I thought it pertinent information."

"Thank you, constable."

"Yes, sir."

Moments later, Mr Perkins had written down and signed his statement (he had waived his right to legal representation), a statement that the DI was now perusing whilst sat across from Mr Perkins in one of the station's four interview rooms.

"So let me see if I've gotten this right? In short, you abducted a member of the public, held them against their will for two days but have since released them. Is that what you're telling us?"

"Yes," replied Mr Perkins, barely able to look at the DI.

"Mr Perkins have you spoken with your wife or had messages from her since returning from your escapades?" queried the DI.

"No," answered a puzzled Mr Perkins. "What's my wife…"

"Mr Perkins, let me assure you that whilst abduction of an adult is a serious felony, it is not, for now, the reason that you are here today. You are here, I'm afraid to say, because" – he paused – "your daughter has not been seen since Friday evening."

"Oh, dear God," gasped Mr Perkins. "Well, what are you doing about it?"

"We have confirmed yours and your wife's whereabouts but we'll need to confirm that with Mr Thompson, although, I can't foresee anyone using that situation as a plausible alibi unless it did actually happen but due diligence and all that. From what you've told me of Mr Thompson, he may have been a person of interest but it appears you've cleared that one from our line of inquiry, although, we will still speak to him as he may know something relevant to the investigation. So, next we'll be speaking to her friends, her boyfriend, her teachers to determine her last known whereabouts and state of mind. We've acquired her cell phone number from your wife but so far we've been unable to locate it. It's either out of battery or it's been powered off. If we're lucky, if it's powered back up again, we'll be able to triangulate her location but so far no luck there."

"Find her. Oh, please God, find her," begged Mr Perkins.

"We'll do our very best Mr Perkins, for now, go home to your wife and wait for your daughter there. If she should arrive home, please inform us," stated DI Jones, as he handed his card to Mr Perkins and guided him out of the building to be escorted home by the same officers who'd driven him previously.

Chapter 32
Monday

Tracey was standing at the door when Bill arrived home, a look of utter despair etched across her face. He could tell what she wanted to know by looking at her.

"No news, I'm afraid. They're headed to the school now."

Closing the door behind him, they wrapped their arms around each other and slumped to the floor under the weight of their tears.

Chapter 33
Monday

Jess had been alone for hours now, since his outburst at her lack of appreciation for him. That had left her with nothing but time to devise a plan. She was a smart girl and determined to find a solution to her predicament. One thing she knew for sure, crying wasn't helping anyone.

It had come to her moments ago, so simple she chastised herself for not figuring it out sooner. Her hands were still free and all that was securing her in place were her ankle restraints. He had changed her clothes but had returned *her* shoes to her feet, and it was the laces in those very shoes that were going to save her.

Chapter 34

Pete

Argh! She's impossible, why can't she see what she means to me? For weeks now, I've watched her, but kept my distance, not wanting to make my move too early, not wanting to scare her away.

How pretty she'd looked at that first lacrosse game, I'd almost wanted to go to her then, settling instead for phoning her just so I could hear her voice, but then he'd shown up, almost walked right past me, and ruined it. She'd been thrilled to see him, Joe, if only she'd look at me that way.

It was at that moment that I decided he didn't deserve her, he didn't treat her with the respect she deserved. Ironic really, if it wasn't for me he wouldn't have had her in the first place and because of me, once again, he wouldn't have her now. That crazy golf game was proof he didn't deserve her, he'd tormented her all night, yet she played along as if it hadn't bothered her – so perfect! Her beauty, both in and out, radiating from her. I had once thought Chrissy was like that but she paled in comparison to Jess. Chrissy, with her constant hair dyeing, craving to be noticed, her lack of regard for schooling or others. She was not Jess; Jess was perfection, supportive of others (I'd seen how much, that night when she'd yelled at me for upsetting Chrissy – but she's not to blame for not understanding my true intent then), she's kind, caring, playful and studious. It was her that deserved to have attention lavished her way.

The gifts had been easy; my neighbour is in her class and I'd simply asked him to deliver them and he did. The notes, letting her know I was thinking about her, each one lovingly written and dropped off at her house, those I'd hand delivered – they were more…more personal.

You looked nice today.

Did you enjoy the chocolates?

You're such a supportive friend, always listening to her drone on. I'm sure you've better things to talk about as you walk to school?

Don't be sad, beautiful, it won't be long now.

But each one, she'd chosen to ignore. "Well you can't ignore me now," he yelled.

She will love me, and if she won't, then…he stormed back into the room.

Chapter 35

Friends and classmates of Jess were interviewed first, each one in turn being summoned to the library for questioning. Nothing had transpired from those conversations except the address of Jess' boyfriend's place of work, they would go there next, but according to Chrissy (Jess' best friend) she wasn't sure if they were still together.

Next was Ms Sharp, the librarian, who apparently was one of the last people to see Jess that day. Jess had been studying here, she told them, and stayed till closing. The only other person on the premises, not counting the caretaker, at the time of closing was Mr Thompson. She believed she'd heard Mr Thompson's voice in the corridor speaking with Jess as she left.

Ordinarily, this would have sent all sorts of alarm bells ringing but thanks to Mr Perkins, they knew that this was a 'red herring', something in the police force known as a fake clue that would lead them nowhere. They'd speak to him nonetheless. Despite his ordeal of the past two days, Mr Thompson was in fact at school and, as it turned out, was rather helpful. He'd mentioned being cut off as he drove out of the school car park by a red corolla; he hadn't thought anything of it at the time, other than how annoyed he was at being cut off, but as he looked in his rear-view mirror, the driver, the young man, was speaking to Jess.

"So this young man, whoever he is, may have been the last person to see Jess that night," stated DI Jones to his team. His phone rang. He answered.

"Okay, perfect Mrs Perkins, thank you for informing us." He hung up.

"What is it? She's back?" asked Constable Hughes.

"No, but apparently she's going to a study group around Lucy's tonight so her parents shouldn't wait up for her."

"This guy's really covering…"

"Sorry to interrupt you but this boy believes he may have some information for you," stated Mr Mc Alistair. "Just tell the officers what you told me, Neil."

"Constable Hughes, check the trace on that phone, maybe we'll get lucky, while I deal with this."

Hughes briskly walked away and began talking down her radio to the tech team back at the station. DI Jones offered the boy a seat and said, "So, son, what is it you've got to tell us?"

"Well," said a nervous and sweating Neil, "when I told you earlier that Jess got that rose and chocolates from her boyfriend, it's cos I thought she did, but I've been speaking to Chrissy and the others at break and they say that she's still with Joe so that means I got it wrong."

Jones had forgotten how quickly information could spread through a school; he flipped through his notes and found what he was looking for.

"Ay, yes, Neil, you stated, and I quote, 'I put a flower on her math seat and left the chocolates by her locker cos her boyfriend asked me to.'"

"Yes, but like I said, I was wrong."

"So, who did give her those gifts?" probed the D.I.

"A guy named Pete Jacobs, he's my neighbour. Am I in trouble? I didn't mean to lie, I mean, I didn't know I was." He was now sweating profusely.

"No, Neil, but for now just go back to class okay. If we need to speak to you further, we'll send someone to get you."

DI Jones ran Pete, Peter, Jacobs, all the names through the DVLAs database – "Bingo!" he said. "A red corolla."

"Hughes, any luck on that phone?"

"Nothing, sir. It's been switched off again."

"Okay, keep me posted. Johnson, get a BOLO (Be on the Lookout) for a red corolla, registration number: BD51 SMR. Tell any responding officer they are to report in only. I repeat, do not engage," declared Jones.

"Right on it, sir," replied Johnson.

"Okay everyone, we believe our perp's name is Peter Jacobs, owner of a red Toyota Corolla and the person responsible for the flower, chocolates and, we believe, notes Miss Perkins received. This guy's been stalking her for weeks. We all know what that means – he's infatuated with her, probably believes that he loves her and that she loves him. Problem there is, the minute his fallacy comes to light that's when Jess' life is at the most risk. Jess really needs to play along with this guy's fantasy but we have no way of letting her know this. She's been with him since Friday night people, so we haven't got much time."

Chapter 36

Reaching forward, Jess removed one of her shoelaces, silently thanking Ms Whitehall for her yoga lessons; she'd never have been able to reach her feet before. She knew that it was a simple matter of physics. By threading the lace though the cable tie all she had to do was repeatedly rub the lace against the tie causing friction. The friction created would cause heat and thus weaken the tie and allow her to break free (that or the shoelace would ignite or snap under the strain of the heat but that is why she'd doubled the lace before threading it through the restraint).

Attentively listening all the while, Jess continued to apply upwards pressure whilst rubbing the shoelace backwards and forwards against the cable tie. It was working, she could feel the heat against her ankle. Minutes later, her right leg was free. Cautiously, she threaded the shoelace through the second binding, the one securing her other leg, and began again but it snapped, despite her precautions the lace had snapped.

She undid the shoelace from her other shoe and began again. She could hear him in the other room, he appeared to be talking to himself, or was there someone else in there, either of whom could return at any moment. She redoubled her efforts and...snap! She was free! Raising herself off the bed, she stepped gingerly towards the window, with trepidation, she placed her hands on the catch praying that it would soundlessly open.

"Don't be sad, beautiful…" – who was he talking to? She didn't wait to find out. She lowered herself from the windowsill and headed away from the building, just moments before Pete had stormed back into the room.

Chapter 37

The building was an abandoned care home, left derelict due to lack of council funds. She remembered her mum speaking about it one morning at breakfast; a shame, she'd said, after reading about it in the local paper. She was local at least, no idea how local on the scheme of things, but she was local, yet far from safe. Her shoes, without their laces, made it difficult to run and right now she wasn't sure where she should be running to, which direction?

* * *

"Sir, we've got a hit. A red Toyota Corolla, registration number: BD51 SMR, was seen yesterday on the Dunstone Byroad. CCTV puts him at the local Dunstone supermarket on Sunday. Having reviewed the store's footage, he bought some food and women's clothing but the last sighting we have is of him heading west back along the Dunstone Byroad. No cameras after that stretch of road, sir. "

"Great job, Johnson. Well, let's get out there. Hughes, you're with me. Johnson, take Fitzpatrick. No black and whites, undercover cars only. I don't want to give this guy the tip off," ordered D. I. Jones.

Most of the police force's vehicles, in fact nearly 50%, were the Battenberg livery of yellow and blue checks but DI Jones was old school and still used the term 'black and whites' referring to some of the older model vehicles the force used.

* * *

"Where are you?" She heard him holler even from this distance away, if she didn't keep moving it wouldn't be long until he'd caught up with her. She removed her shoes, holding them as a makeshift weapon if needed and ran.

* * *

"What do you mean, Pete's got her?" asked a perplexed Joe.

"Pete, he's been like, stalking her or whatever and giving her gifts and stuff," explained a tormented Chrissy.

Joe punched the bonnet of the car he'd been working on, leaving a noticeable dent.

"I'll kill him," he raged, dialling his number.

"Hey mate, can't talk now, I'm a little busy," answered Pete, after taking Joe's call.

"Where is she Pete? What have you done to her?"

"Who? What are you talking 'bout?" asked Pete feigning ignorance.

"You know exact..." but Pete had already hung up.

Collecting his keys from the nearby rack, Joe opened the car and told Chrissy to get in as he started the engine.

"Won't your boss care that you're leaving work – and the dent in that car?" she asked, looking once more at the dented car left in Joe's wake.

"Nah, my dad owns the place and I'll buff out that dent, it'll be good as new."

"Okay, so where are we going?"

"To Pete's house."

"But won't the police have already been there?" stated Chrissy.

"Yea, probably, but we'll go there anyway, maybe they'll tell me something that they didn't tell the police."

* * *

Jess raced forwards but then stopped abruptly. She'd chosen badly, it was a cul-de-sac – she was trapped. The only way out was to retrace her steps, but surely that'd mean bumping into Pete. Normally, she wasn't the type to disturb others but she was desperate, she began pounding on the doors of local residents.

* * *

Which way did you go? You're not getting away from me that easily.

Chapter 38

Mrs Perkins sat stoically on the floral armchair in her living room, drinking yet another cup of strong tea. Jenny, the 43-year-old FSO (Family Support Officer), had added yet more sugar to this cup to help absorb the shock and finally, she believed it was working as she monitored the almost motionless Mrs Perkins. Mr Perkins, on the other hand, was troubling her, he had been pacing the room for almost an hour now and she wasn't sure how much longer she could placate him.

Jenny had watched many families over the years go through similar situations. First, there's denial, where the family refuses to accept what's happening – no, there must be some mistake, it can't be their son, daughter, etc. Then anger, whereby the family lash out at the police initially and then turn on each other. These stages had both happened here but rather than lash out at his wife, Mr Perkins had merely accepted blame, whether because he couldn't defend himself and his absence or because he truly believed he was to blame, Jenny couldn't ascertain. Next would come bargaining and this is what Jenny wanted to avoid at all costs; she knew from experience that what Mr Perkins would bargain for was to be allowed to leave his home and search for his daughter – this, she could not let happen.

Chapter 39

Jess had knocked on at least five doors but all went unanswered. She had heard a dog yipping behind one door and held her breath in hope but it, too, had gone unanswered. She feared that at any moment now, Pete would appear and drag her back to where she'd been held captive, or would he do worse, angered by her escape. She needed a different plan, she needed to hide.

The cul-de-sac had semi-detached houses lining each side of the street, many with gates leading to back gardens. She could try those but wouldn't he be expecting that? Instead, she chose to sandwich herself behind a parked car and two wheelie bins in someone's driveway. *Please, God, let this do,* she prayed.

Chapter 40

"Hey, Aunty Pam, how are you?" asked a concerned Joe.

"I suppose you've heard the news? They gave me a right grillin', those police officers, but I told 'em, I don't know nothin'," she said, as she made her way back to her kitchen to sit down.

"Let me make you a mug of tea. Milk and two sugars, right?"

"You're a good lad, Joe," she replied, patting his hand. Only then did she notice the girl Joe had with him. "Chrissy love, how are ya?"

"Well, not too good really; my best friend's missing!" She answered even more harshly than she'd meant to.

"Of course, of course. I'm sorry. I don't know what to tell ya both, I knew nothin' of this." She placed her head in her hands and wept. Joe knew she was telling the truth and worse still, that she blamed herself for her son's actions.

"It's not your fault," Joe soothed. "He's an adult now, he's responsible for his own actions. Whatever he's done, that's on him."

Pam looked up for a brief moment, directing her gaze at Joe. "He'll go to prison, won't he?"

Joe didn't have the heart to reply, so instead said, "Hush now, let's not worry about that now. Let's just drink this tea," and he handed her the freshly made mug of tea.

Chapter 41

Pete appeared within minutes of her hiding. She couldn't see him exactly, more sensed him and she heard footsteps coming down the path. At the moment, from the sound of his footfalls, he was on the opposite side of the street. She presumed he was doing what she had earlier – searched. She imagined him searching gardens and back gates and many a time, she heard the rattle of a gate followed by a thumping sound, she assumed that when the gate hadn't opened he had jumped to spy over the fence for her. It wouldn't be long now until he was on the same side of the street as her, would he be thorough? Would he find her? Her heart stopped when she heard a voice.

Chapter 42

DI Jones and his team had been circulating Dunstone for nearly 20 minutes now, they were about to double back and search farther afield when Hughes shouted, "Woah, hold up. Reverse. There." She pointed. DI Jones drove in and parked beside the red Toyota Corolla. It was the one they were looking for, registration confirmed it.

"Wasn't this that old council care home," asked Hughes.

"Yes, so here's what we're going to do."

They were to venture towards the main door as regular members of the public, coming to see a family friend, unaware of the building's closure. "Be on high alert," the DI had told her. "We don't know what this guy's capable of."

They radioed the other members of the team informing them of their location but for now they were to hold their positions. Casually, they entered through the already open front door and made their way methodically through each and every room. They discovered trace evidence of Jess having been there: her phone, her uniform, book bag but the building was empty.

DI Jones telephoned the Perkins' home and Mr Perkins grabbed the receiver.

"Yes? I mean…Hello."

"Mr Perkins, this is DI Jones."

"Have you got her? Is she safe?" interjected Mr Perkins.

"Mr Perkins, she's escaped. We've not got her yet but she's a resilient girl and she's fighting, all of which are good signs. Can you please pass the phone to Jenny?"

"Yes of course," replied a relieved Mr Perkins.

DI Jones relayed the same information to Jenny that he had to Mr Perkins but added, "We still don't have him, Jenny." He didn't have to say anything more. Jenny knew that this meant the girl wasn't out of danger yet, he'd be pursuing her, but for now her parents had hope.

Chapter 43

"Can I help you?" It was a man's voice, but an older man and he didn't appear to be speaking to her.

"Oh, hello, yes maybe you can. I'm looking for my sister, we got into an argument and she ran off. I've been sent to find her so that we can all leave again, our family that is. Oh and to apologise, of course."

It disgusted Jess how easily Pete could lie.

"I've not seen anyone around here all week," he said.

"Then I'll just keep looking," replied Pete, anger rising in his voice.

"This is a neighbourhood watch area, young man. I saw you looking in those gardens and peering over fences. If you don't move on, I'll have no choice but to phone the police," said the older man, standing his ground.

Pete weighed his options and chose to leave, not because he was threatened by this frail old man; not because he thought the police would be after him, he'd covered his tracks there but because if he was having to answer the questions of a police officer, then it would allow Jess more time to properly escape and that, he wasn't prepared to risk.

"Thanks for nothing," Pete rebuked as he turned and walked away.

The man had stood there the whole time watching Pete leave and then longer still, before calling to her. Jess timidly rose from behind the bins. "You knew I was there?"

"Yes. I knew you were there. I'd watched you just as I'd watched him. You looked lost whereas he looked menacing. Come in, come in," he ushered, as he quickly shut the door to his home behind them both.

Jess shook uncontrollably and a steady stream of tears flowed down her cheeks. The man eyed the girl standing before him, clearly emotional and barefoot.

"My dear girl, what has he done to you? Please, come sit. Can I call someone for you?"

By the time the police had arrived, Jess was calmer and less jittery. Every sound within the house had made her jump but Mr Jeffries had assured her it was just an old house. That was his name, Mr Jeffries, the blessed man who had saved her. The man whom she would be eternally grateful to and from now on would do anything for – she owed him her life, she was sure of it.

She was reluctant to leave him. He'd made her feel safe, had been a safe haven amidst the storm but she knew she must. Her parents had been informed and they were to meet her at the police station, she was going home.

Chapter 44

DI Jones personally escorted Jess back to the station, accompanied by DC Hughes, where she was reunited with her family. The rest of the team were still on the lookout for Pete. The black and whites were now deployed too and a photograph had been issued to all involved. Later, a statement would be released to the press and a nationwide search would begin.

* * *

Pam had texted her son after she'd been informed of the proceedings and was now being charged with obstruction of justice and impeding a police investigation. Her son had since gone to ground and the police had no leads.

* * *

Joe couldn't blame his aunt; he had seen how guilty and responsible she'd felt. Her texting Pete was her redemption – her last act in helping her son as it was clear to her that she'd failed him up until now. Why else would he have done what he'd done?

Personally, he hoped that the police would find Pete and arrest him but he'd never admit that to his family. As for Jess, he was pleased she was safe but nothing more. Even before this had started she'd behaved, reacted immaturely. He didn't need games, didn't need to justify himself for the actions of others, so they were done but he wished her the best and would still be there for her if she needed.

* * *

Mr Perkins was cautioned about his behaviour but since Mr Thompson wasn't pressing charges it was no longer a police matter. He was told to go home and look after his family and to leave police matters to the police.

* * *

Mr Thompson was promoted to Head of Department after the retirement of Mr Flynn, which had been the whisperings and silences he'd encountered at school. Staff had known but weren't allowed to tell him. He couldn't be happier.

* * *

Jess was now seeing a psychiatrist. She hadn't wanted to at first but it was helping. She couldn't talk to her parents about what had happened, they were worrying and fussing about her too much as it was and Chrissy, well, she couldn't talk to her. Pete was her ex, and Joe, well…Pete had cost her a lot but he hadn't cost her Joe, she realised; that was on her.

So, she talked to the psychiatrist every Tuesday, and cried, then talked some more and afterwards Chrissy would meet her for ice cream and they'd laugh and discuss clothes and school and their futures, you know, normal stuff – life had to go on.